Frog Went A-Courting

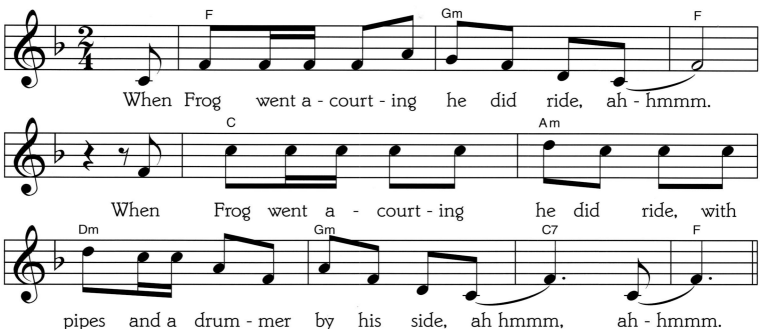

When Frog went a - court - ing he did ride, ah - hmmm.

When Frog went a - court - ing he did ride, with

pipes and a drum - mer by his side, ah hmmm, ah - hmmm.

Continue with the same melody for the rest of the verses. For a simpler version, play an F major chord throughout.

Well Frog and his love went off to France.
So ends our story but starts their romance.

He yowled, "I'LL PUT A STOP TO THAT!"

When, "MEE-OW," growled the quick Tomcat.

ACT FIVE

As evening came Frog coaxed his wife
with the prettiest tune he'd played in his life.

He laughed and said, "Just came for cake."

Even Sir Turtle rowed across the lake.

Madam Moth had much to say.
She gave the guests a special day.

They ate their fill with Chef Raccoon,
who served the feast with a silver spoon.

to face a bug who talked and talked.

Down the aisle Miss Mouse she walked

cut from the finest silks in town.

Jolly Miss Mole made the wedding gown,

ACT THREE

The old gray rat was quick to her door
and Frog was the dandy he was before.

"Charmed," said Rat and gave his consent.
Next you'll hear how the wedding went.

without the consent of my Uncle Rat."

But Miss Mouse sighed, "I can't do that

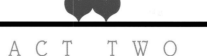

ACT TWO

Up they rode to Grand Mouse Hall;
Frog's pipes ringing in a rousing call.

Miss Mouse hurried to her balcony
to hear Frog singing, "Will you marry me?"

his buckled boots shone black as jet.

So high upon his mount Frog sat,

When Frog went a-courting he did ride
with pipes and a drummer by his side.

CAST OF CHARACTERS

FROG - a dandy about town and player of pipes

SHREW - a dutiful servant and rousing good drummer

MISS MOUSE - a kind and respectful fair maiden

RAT - a shrewd yet devoted uncle

MISS MOLE - a nearsighted but still excellent seamstress

REVEREND BUG - a jovial orator with much to say

MADAM MOTH - a lover of finery and grand affairs

CHEF RACCOON - a genius in the kitchen

OLD TURTLE - a pleasant and good-humored fellow

THE TOMCAT - a fierce critic of musical talent

Thank you to all whose guidance and encouragement
have led me gently into the bright light of books:
Patty G., Tracy G., Barbara L., Larry R.,
Tim G., Kent B., & John K.
- D.C.

Text and illustrations copyright © 1998 by Dominic Catalano
All rights reserved

Published by Caroline House
Boyds Mills Press, Inc.
A Highlights Company
815 Church Street
Honesdale, Pennsylvania 18431
Printed in Hong Kong

Publisher Cataloging-in-Publication Data
Catalano, Dominic
Frog went a-courting : a muscial play in six acts / retold and
illustrated by Dominic Catalano.—1st.ed. [32] p. : col. ill. : cm.
Summary: A picture book retelling of the traditional folk song.
ISBN 1-56397-637-4
1. Folk songs, English—United States—Juvenile literature.
[1. Folk songs, English—United States.] I. Title.
782.42162—dc21   1998   AC   CIP
Library of Congress Catalog Card Number 97-777908

First edition, 1998
Book designed by Dominic Catalano
The text of this book is set in 24pt. Belwe Mono Let Plain
The illustrations are done in pastels.

10 9 8 7 6 5 4 3 2

The Highland Minstrel Players
Proudly Present

Frog Went A-Courting

A Musical Play in Six Acts

RETOLD & ILLUSTRATED BY

DOMINIC CATALANO

Boyds Mills Press

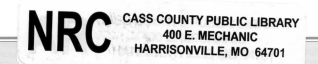

"Ladies and Gentlemen . . ."

Frog Went A-Courting